$\mathscr{S}$OULMATE

JONATHAN LOVEJOY

Jonathan Lovejoy

SOULMATE

Roanoke River Bride

Jonathan Lovejoy

Cover Art: *Study of a Woman's Head*, 1898
William Adolphe Bouguereau (1825-1905)

ISBN-10: 0692318852
ISBN-13: 978-0692318850

For the Lonely

Introduction

The tragedy of human existence is Fate. And this, to the passing of the proverbial ships in the night, when the energy of a meeting unrequited is sparked between them. And these two souls disembark upon a distant shore, as far apart as east is from west, where never the twain shall meet. They wander the wilderness in two separate Hells on Earth, meeting other lonely souls along the way. Marrying, giving in marriage. Eating, drinking, and being merry on the long journey home. Touching one, two, or three of these tragic spirits in the futility of union, where there is nothing but a sea of lost tranquility that awaits, an ocean of discord that crashes as the sounding sea.

Five, ten, twenty years of this storm may pass. Until one day, one dreary afternoon and night, as the spark of lightning flashes—to roll the thunder of sorrow across their landscape of grieving—they remember the eyes of one that they have met before, the spark and flash of memory that once trembled their Soul. When the Mate that was born to them by nature was captured by the Winds of Time, and whisked so coldly away from the warmth of love, joy and peace. Where the fountain of their love flows waters of Tranquility, and the daily bread of Compassion would have drifted down to them like manna from heaven.

Jonathan Lovejoy

Jonathan Lovejoy

SOULMATE

or

"Roanoke River Bride"

Jonathan Lovejoy

Such is the grandest music among us—
Poets...
Such are the wildest thoughts among us—
Composers...

Roanoke River Bride

I

Jonathan Lovejoy

1

My soulmate fades into a memory
Twenty years of loveliness I recall
A spark passed through me like a flash of light—
When I passed her by in the University Hall

Never a cross word there would have been
Great lovers in their marital bed
Love and an understanding heart—
Are the fountains by which their souls are fed

My soulmate fades into a memory
Twenty years of loveliness I recall
I saw a life of peace and prosperity pass on—
When I passed her by in the University Hall

My heart lifts across the miles
Down east—by the Roanoke River bend
Where I lost my soulmate twenty years ago
And where I hope to find her once again

Past the love that was lost—the river flows
To torture my soul with what'll never be
A future of great lovers lost in the wind—
To burden my soul with misery

I dare not look into the evening day
At twilight—when the sun has come and gone
Because there, her eyes might gaze upon me—
From dusk until the morning dawn

She lifts my heart across the miles
Down east—by the Roanoke River bend
Where I lost my soulmate 20 years ago
And where I found her once again

My soulmate met me in the evening day
At the edge of the field of Perpetuity
We watched the sunlight fade away
Until only the evening star was left to see

Above the twilight of all mankind
This star shines in celestial beauty
Over the forests and fields of our hearts and minds
His infinitesimal ingenuity

Two souls adrift in the evening day
Take hands in the fading summer's light
Strolling quietly along their way—
Love and Beauty in the coming night

*S*omewhere in my heart, my soulmate lives
Bestowed to me in the Evening Day
Love and kindness unsurpassed
A sweet and understanding way

We stroll the banks of the Roanoke River
Hand in hand down Sunset Way
With nary a cross word in our hearts—
As the light of sunset fades away

Twenty years and twenty five miles down east
My soulmate walks in the Evening Day
Lost to me except in my heart—
Because a calling came and took me away

I saw my soulmate at the door
In our Twilight Cabin by the Sea
Love and kindness such as never was before—
To bathe our souls in tranquility

A stranger greeted her loveliness
At the doorway of our happy home
I felt his soul go green with envy—
At the beauty of just her sweetness alone

Love gathers our dinner in the Evening Day
Left by the stranger along their way
Who saw sweetness at the door of tranquility—
In our Twilight Cabin by the Sea

My helpmate now must hold the place
Where my soulmate would have been
Despite her calling to worldliness—
And her rendezvous with lust and sin

But in the summer breeze over the grassy field
The goldfinch sings a melody
About the beauty of what love was lost—
And a score of years in misery

Our hearts drift down the Roanoke River
The true love of my soul and me
Where we would have made a happy home—
In a twilight cabin by the sea

7

My spirit is full but my soul is empty
At the field by Ardmore Village Wood
As my soulmate drifts a field aplenty
Somewhere in the world I never could

This helpmate can never a soulmate be
Too racked with lust and carnality
A heart of love grown icy cold—
While my true love haunts my memory

By the wings of this goldfinch elegy
Her voice sings over the grassy sea
As the earth turns toward the Evening Day—
My soulmate joins her soul to me

My soulmate rose again from the East
From the banks of our Roanoke River bend
Where we live our lives in tranquility—
With Love and Peace that has no end

Loveliness in the evening day
With our bright and evening star in sight
We take hands beyond the setting sun
Under the star that rules the coming night

By the banks of the Roanoke River bend
Down east—my soulmate calls to me again
A soul of Love and Joy and Peace—
And our tranquility that has no end

9

She came to me in the evening day
The ghost of someone I never knew
A spirit of love and understanding—
Took my hand under the fading nighttime blue

This half moon glows over our resolve
This union of souls never meant to be
A lifetime of happiness gone away
When I saw her turn and walk away from me

The spirit of my soulmate lives in me
When twilight becomes the evening day
From Roanoke River to Ardmore Village Wood—
To banish the loneliness in my heart away

10

I felt my soulmate in a cooling breeze
In the balm of a warm summer's day
She brushed through my heart and through my soul—
Drifting along her merry way

To remind me of 25 miles down east
And the years I lost in love and peace
Having only pondered what substance is tranquility—
And a life unantagonized into a raging beast

"Nary a cross word" she tells me again
Is the paradise that our lives would have been
My soulmate touched me on a cooling breeze—
To carry me aloft upon a cool summer wind

11

The Holy Spirit showed me my soulmate again
Along the forest and fields of a distant ride
On the country outskirts of my hometown—
As the breeze blows through hair of silken brown

A smile to banish a mist of sorrow
Prettiness resurrected in every tomorrow
To remind me that there is only joy—
And two souls together in harmony

We cruise the streets of my hometown
Hand in hand, my soulmate and me
Our hearts heavy with our journey through the evening day—
To our home in the twilight by the sea

12

Peace and an understanding heart
Are what my soulmate would have been
Not the carrion I've been forced to live—
With the woman I was cursed to marry

A disgusting, disturbing, dreadful marriage
Is the curse under which I've been called
Twenty two years of burning Hell—
Is the alcohol splashed wound from this razor claw

So the memory of my soulmate is sacred
A gift from God for the pain I'm in
Of the heart that waits for me down east—
In the twilight by the Roanoke River Bend

II

13

*M*y soulmate touched me in the evening day
At our twilight cabin by the sea
After we watched the sunset fade away—
In crimson amber tranquility

A kiss bestowed by the crescent moon
Two flames colored by a happy tune
Love lifts and carries us thru the night—
An erotic explosion in lover's delight

To lovers underneath the crescent moon
Two souls colored by a happy tune
At the place where our tranquility has no end—
Our twilight stroll by the Roanoke River bend

14

A letter from my soulmate came in the mail
In my most fervent wish and dream
A letter beseeching me to come to her—
By the banks of the Roanoke River fish and stream

Fluffy white clouds in the noonday sun
Beckon her and me to walk again
To laugh and talk and have some fun—
Until our lifetime of prosperity comes in

My soulmate sent me a letter in the mail
Beckoning me to come her way
Down east nearby the Roanoke River—
For a stroll that lasts until the evening day

I wish that I had married my soulmate
I wish that I had been happy
Days unmarked by sorrow or tears—
Years unclouded by rage or fear

Compassion clouded by lack of understanding
Is the punishment by which my time is wrought
Married to a woman with a heart of stone—
Except toward silliness and bitter wars to be fought

My soulmate has an understanding heart
A soul of wisdom to say the least
She waits for me by the Roanoke River—
Across the years and twenty five miles down east

I looked my soulmate in the eye today
In the lot of Lost Hope and Shattered Dreams
She waits with me at the edge of loneliness
As the barrier of love and joy in between

In the world long past the setting sun
On the far edge of the approaching night
Two souls united in understanding—
Take hands in the fading autumn light

From twenty years and twenty five miles down east
A deep and abiding love will stay
Sharing a kiss and a warm embrace—
As the earth turns toward the evening day

17

*M*y soulmate walked with me in the moonlight
This, the light of the crescent Harvest Moon
I understand, she said, *all the pain you've been through—*
I'll die before I cause a moment's pain for me and you

Unable to speak, I take her hand
Under the Roanoke Crescent Moon
As long as it's you and me, she said—
Until the day both of us are dead

Two soulmates under the Harvest Moon
Take hands—to never again be alone
They walk together by the Roanoke River—
Until the Angel of the Lord comes to call them home

My soulmate walked with me in the Evening Day
In the field by the Roanoke River Wood
Immersed in love and understanding—
More profound than I thought what we ever could

Gazing the light over the Western Rim
Amber as far as the eye can see
As we put our arms around each other—
To finish our stroll in tranquility

Two soulmates adrift in the Evening Day
Spirits united, come what may
In deeper love than we thought what we ever could
In the field by the Roanoke River Wood

19

My soulmate lives in the evening day
Down by the Roanoke River way
When the sunset rests below the horizon
In amber crested naiveté

Warm feelings in the cold November wind
By the light of the evening star's delight
With no painful memories left to mend
In the heart of Autumn's approaching night

She lives with me in the evening day
My soulmate—in Love's Humility
Unable to fathom what possibility
Of what love there is still meant to be

20

I saw my soulmate stroll the field of hay
By where the cardinals, bluebirds and butterflies play
After the Autumn leaves have died and gone away—
As the world turns toward the evening day

Pray tell, by what Spirit—strolling there
Such wandering gaze and skin so fair
Of what earthly concern we hath nary a care—
Except to love our hearts and souls laid bare

I walked with my soulmate in the field of hay
Near our cabin by the Roanoke River Way
What spark doth flash my soul when she takes my hand—
Beneath the star that shines above the evening day

21

My soulmate waits for me Down East
In the heart of yellow leaf tobacco country
Her spirit beckons me from across the miles—
To protect my soul from misery

A soul of understanding lost to me
The power of a stroll in a starry night
The beauty of a flower in a summer field—
The glory of a life without bitterness and spite

Down East—my soulmate waits for me
Our souls' briefest misery
Love and Understanding lost in the wind—
Like a stroll at Cape Hatteras by the sea

22

My soulmate walked with me in the cold north wind
On our winter trail through the falling snow
She warms my heart by the Roanoke River Bend—
When icy breezes begin to blow

In awe of a world covered in snowy white
Beneath gloomy skies of winter gray
Unable to fathom even the playful fight—
In the snows of the approaching evening day

Praying our winter souls to keep
When icy Roanoke River breezes blow
An embrace that endeavors our hearts to weep—
On our trail through the wind and falling snow

23

My soulmate stood with me in the rain and winter
At the door of our cabin of tranquility
Boldly we step into the cold and rain—
To marvel the rainy winter wind and sea

Two hearts aflame in the rain and mist
Warming one another in the cold and gray
Shocked by the spark of her sudden kiss—
On my cheek in this cold and rainy day

Souls ignited from fires within
My soulmate touches me in the winter wind
In the lawn by our cabin of tranquility
In awe of the rainy winter wind and sea

24

*M*y soulmate came to me on Christmas Eve
By the light of our Carolina Christmas Tree
As our gazes are affixed to Treetop Tall—
At the angel of peace and tranquility

On our stroll through the forest of Christmas Trees
In the southern Appalachian Mountain Wood
Our souls reach out to this Frasier Fir
In what manner we've forever understood

Our hearts beckon us to Treetop Tall
In the fading light of Christmas Eve
As my soulmate and me look to the Angel—
In our cabin of love and tranquility

25

My soulmate cruised the dinner trail with me
Hungry for love in the evening day
Somewhere lavender and amber Down East—
To talk and dine every care and concern away

Spiritual and intellectual stimulation
Our sweet and easy slice of pie
Wary of nary a confrontation—
That would cause our love and tranquility to die

My soulmate dines with me Down East
While the cold winter light begins to fade away
Hungry for our nighttime's future embrace—
As the earth turns toward the Evening Day

$\mathcal{M}y$ soulmate heard the chiming of the whistle train
Down East—by the Roanoke River Way
We walk the streets of our hometown
Hand in hand in the Light of Day

She turns her head toward a distant horizon
Somewhere beyond what roads and buildings we see
To a field of grass that blows in the wind—
Near our cabin of love and tranquility

Hand in hand on our stroll Down East
In the town by Roanoke River Way
My soulmate hears the chiming of the whistle train—
Calling us home in the Evening Day

We rolled to the lights of earthly progression
On the night of Christmas—my soulmate and me
The countryside glowed in starlight beauty
In colors as far as the eye can see

Having disembarked our rolling winter chariot
To marvel such beauty the earth hath seen
The colors of Salvation, Redemption and Creation—
In the spirits of white and red and green

Angels in flight over our Christmas night
To alight comfort upon my soulmate and me
As we hold hands by the lighted countryside—
Burdened by Love's Humility

My soulmate and me in the heart of Creation
In our winter cabin of tranquility
In awe of the power from Almighty God—
Adrift in the snows of gentility

As these arctic breezes endeavor to blow
From the Appalachians to Down East they go
The Winter Wind howls the world outside we know—
To bury the landscape in ice and snow

Warm in the heart of winter creation
By the icy Roanoke River Way
She takes my hand by the twilight window—
While we watch the snow fall in the evening day

My soulmate lives in the heart of Redemption

In our cabin of winter tranquility

Our hearts touched by our Lord and Savior—

Our souls burdened by Humility

As the shepherds who abided in the fields

Humbled when the heavenly hosts appeared

The love of Christ hath burdened our hearts to tears—

With no more sorrow or loneliness to fear

Languished together in the heart of Redemption

In our home of winter tranquility

Love's Humility strengthens our embrace—

Warm in our cabin by the sea

30

My soulmate and me are one in Salvation

The Holy Spirit in Love's Humility

We wait for the Lord to carry us home—

From our cabin of winter tranquility

Love and an understanding heart

Are the fountains by which our souls were fed

Led by the Holy Spirit of God—

To make joy and peace our daily bread

The morning star rises in the East

When winter's cold begins to fade away

I rest with my soulmate in eternity—

When the star shines above the Evening Day

31

My soulmate is born again to my memory
To protect my heart from misery
As she rides with me under cloak of night—
In the calm of our New Year's reverie

Silhouettes of old houses passing by
Dark'ned memories from lives unknown
She wonders with me what nature of pain they knew—
Knowing we will never again be alone

We ride somewhere in the starlight Down East
Through the nighttime cold of New Year's Eve
Protecting one another on the Road of Peace—
From the spirits that endeavor a heart to grieve

My soulmate lives in my hometown
Down East—by Roanoke River Way
She haunts the roads of my ghostly passing—
By the forests and fields of love, I pray

Along the back roads and streets we ride
Watching the countryside passing by
Her loveliness beams my soul with pride
That I must resist these tears to cry

From whenceforth cometh this tranquility!
What spirit doth bond my soulmate and me?
With nary a cross word in this serenity—
On the ride to our cabin by the wind and sea

33

My soulmate met me on the Eastern Rim
On the eve of their understanding of the Armageddon Hymn
To watch the earth turn toward the morning day
Where love and tranquility have come to stay

Intellectual curiosity
Spiritual luminosity
Waits for us at the end of this age—
In the sunrise of his grand and Holy grandiosity

My soulmate waits with me on the Eastern Rim
On the eve of their understanding of the Armageddon Hymn
Still lost in the heart of Love's Humility
At the end of the age in the Dove's Tranquility

34

My soulmate loves me on the Western Rim
In their tragic understanding of the Armageddon Hymn
Carmen Coletti is *Elizabeth* to them
When the Second Coming of Christ is her musical gem

My Dearest Soulmate—I pledge my heart to thee
Unburden my heart by thine love for me
As this end-of-the-world comet emblazens our twilight by and bye
She takes my hand underneath the star where our Redemption draweth nigh

My soulmate loves me on the Western Rim
In their tragic understanding of the Armageddon Hymn
Where Love's Humility has come to stay
By the Dove's Tranquility in the Evening Day

ABOUT THE AUTHOR

Jonathan Lovejoy is a graduate of the University of North Carolina at Greensboro, with a B.A. in Religious Studies, and a graduate of Liberty Baptist Theological Seminary at Liberty University, with an M.A. in Theological Studies. He currently lives in Winston Salem, North Carolina.

For more info on the author's life and career, visit jonathanlovejoy.com.